The Clc Slide Show

Story by Sally Cowan
Illustrations by Christina Miesen

Contents

Chapter 1	The Photo Project	3
Chapter 2	Where Is the Camera?	4
Chapter 3	No Photos	9
Chapter 4	Lots of Photos	14

Chapter 1

The Photo Project

Asha had been at her new school for a week.
She liked school very much.
She had even made friends with a girl
called Lucy.

One day, their teacher, Ms Wills, said,
"I want you all to take photos
of the people and things around you.
Then, we will make a slide show
that your families can come and watch."

Chapter 2
Where Is the Camera?

After school, Asha looked for the camera.
She wanted to start taking photos.
She hunted everywhere for it,
but she couldn't find it.

Her family had moved into their new house
a week ago.
There were still some boxes left to unpack.

"Where is our camera, Mum?" asked Asha.

"Hmm," said Mum. "It must be here somewhere."

Asha and Mum looked through the boxes,
but they still couldn't find the camera.

Just then, Dad came in the front door.
"What are you looking for?" he asked.

"Our camera," said Asha.
"I need it to take photos
for a slide show at school.
Do you know where it is, Dad?"

"Don't you remember?" said Dad.
"I gave the camera to Kofi,
to take on his school camp."

Kofi was Asha's big brother.

"Oh, no!" said Asha.
"He won't be back for days!"

Chapter 3

No Photos

At school the next day, Asha was very upset.

She talked to Ms Wills.
"Don't worry, Asha," said Ms Wills.
"If you can't do the project,
you can just look at everyone else's photos."

Asha didn't feel any better.
She wanted to take photos of her family, too.

At lunch time, Asha was sitting with Lucy and some other children.

"I'm going to take photos of my dancing class and my dog!" said Lucy.

"My football team is playing on Sunday," said Marco.
"I'll take photos of my team!"

"We are going on a fishing trip this Saturday," said Pippa.
"I'll take photos of the biggest fish I catch!"

"What about you, Asha?" asked Lucy.

Asha put down her lunch box
and rushed over behind a tree.
She was crying.

Lucy followed her.
"Asha, are you all right?" asked Lucy.

"I can't take any photos
for the slide show!" she cried.
"My brother has taken our camera
to his school camp."

Lucy suddenly smiled.

"My big sister has a camera," she said.

"She might lend it to you.

I'll ask her later, and let you know."

Chapter 4
Lots of Photos

Lucy's big sister was happy to lend Asha her camera.

Asha took a photo of her new house.

She took a photo of her new bedroom. And she took a photo of her mum and dad at a picnic in the park.

She even took a photo of herself with Lucy.

Asha had lots of photos!

She felt very proud
on the day of the slide show,
as her photos came up on the big screen.

Later, Ms Wills said, "Well done, Asha.
Everyone liked your photos!"

"Thanks to Lucy
and her big sister!" said Asha.